P9-DNO-916

the MONSTER at the end of this book

By Jon Stone

Illustrated by Michael Smollin

A GOLDEN BOOK • NEW YORK

Copyright © 1971 by Sesame Workshop. Copyright renewed 1999 by Sesame Workshop. All rights reserved under International and Pan-American Copyright Conventions. Published in the United States by Golden Books, an imprint of Random House Children's Books, a division of Random House, Inc., New York, and simultaneously in Canada by Random House of Canada Limited, Toronto, in conjunction with Sesame Workshop. Sesame Street, Sesame Workshop, and their logos are trademarks and service marks of Sesame Workshop. Golden Books, A Golden Book, A Little Golden Book, the G colophon, and the distinctive gold spine are registered trademarks of Random House, Inc. Originally published in 1971 by Golden Books.

Library of Congress Control Number: 2002112774
ISBN: 0-307-01085-6
www.goldenbooks.com
PRINTED IN CHINA
Second Little Golden Book Edition 2003
10 9 8 7 6 5 4 3 2 1

WHAT DID THAT SAY?

On the first page, what did that say? Did that say there will be a Monster at the end of this book ???
IT DID?
Oh, I am so scared of Monsters!!!

SHH

Listen, I have an idea. If you do not turn **any pages**, we will never get to the end of this book.
And that is good, because there is a **Monster** at the end of this book.
So please do not turn the page.

YOU TURNED THE PAGE!

Maybe you do not understand. You see, turning pages will bring us to the end of this book, and there is a **Monster** at the end of this book...

...but **this** will stop you from turning pages. See? I am tying the pages together so you cannot....

YOU TURNED ANOTHER PAGE!
You do not know what you are doing to me!
now...
STOP TURNING PAGES!

THERE! I, Grover, am nailing this page to the next one so that you will not be able to turn it, and we will not get any closer to the Monster at the end of this book.

BONK BAM
BING
KLON
BONK
WOOD

A

ALL RIGHT!
ALL RIGHT!
ALL RIGHT!
Do you know that every time you turn another page . . . you not only get us closer to the MONSTER at the end of this book, but you make
a terrible mess!

This will stop you from turning pages. A heavy, thick, solid, strong **brick wall**. I would just like to see you **TRY** to turn this page.

GLUE

Do you know that
you are very strong ?

The next page is the end of this book, and there is a MONSTER at the end of this book.
Oh, I am so SCARED!

PLEASE
do not turn the page.
PLEASE
PLEASE
PLEASE

Well, look at that! This is the end of the book, and the only one here is ...
ME
I, lovable, furry old
GROVER,
am the Monster at the end of this book.
And you were so SCARED!

THE
I told you and told you there was nothing to be afraid of.

Oh, I am so embarrassed....